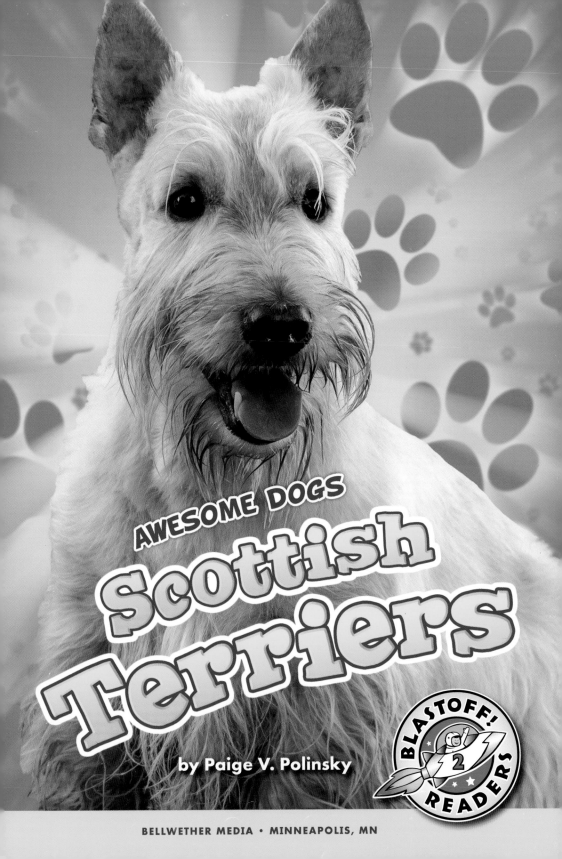

AWESOME DOGS

Scottish Terriers

by Paige V. Polinsky

BLASTOFF! READERS

2

BELLWETHER MEDIA • MINNEAPOLIS, MN

Note to Librarians, Teachers, and Parents:

Blastoff! Readers are carefully developed by literacy experts and combine standards-based content with developmentally appropriate text.

Level 1 provides the most support through repetition of high-frequency words, light text, predictable sentence patterns, and strong visual support.

Level 2 offers early readers a bit more challenge through varied simple sentences, increased text load, and less repetition of high-frequency words.

Level 3 advances early-fluent readers toward fluency through increased text and concept load, less reliance on visuals, longer sentences, and more literary language.

Level 4 builds reading stamina by providing more text per page, increased use of punctuation, greater variation in sentence patterns, and increasingly challenging vocabulary.

Level 5 encourages children to move from "learning to read" to "reading to learn" by providing even more text, varied writing styles, and less familiar topics.

Whichever book is right for your reader, Blastoff! Readers are the perfect books to build confidence and encourage a love of reading that will last a lifetime!

This edition first published in 2019 by Bellwether Media, Inc.

No part of this publication may be reproduced in whole or in part without written permission of the publisher. For information regarding permission, write to Bellwether Media, Inc., Attention: Permissions Department, 6012 Blue Circle Drive, Minnetonka, MN 55343.

Library of Congress Cataloging-in-Publication Data

Names: Polinsky, Paige V., author.
Title: Scottish Terriers / by Paige V. Polinsky.
Description: Minneapolis, MN : Bellwether Media, Inc., 2019. | Series:
   Blastoff! Readers. Awesome Dogs | Audience: Age 5-8. | Audience: Grade K
   to 3. | Includes bibliographical references and index.
Identifiers: LCCN 2017056572 (print) | LCCN 2018005280 (ebook) | ISBN
   9781626177949 (hardcover : alk. paper) | ISBN 9781681035338 (ebook)
Subjects: LCSH: Scottish terrier–Juvenile literature.
Classification: LCC SF429.S4 (ebook) | LCC SF429.S4 P65 2019 (print) | DDC
   636.755–dc23
LC record available at https://lccn.loc.gov/2017056572

Editor: Rebecca Sabelko   Designer: Jeffrey Kollock

Printed in the United States of America, North Mankato, MN.

Table of Contents

What Are Scottish Terriers?

Scottish Terriers are small, **sturdy** dogs. They are known for their bravery.

People often call them Scotties.

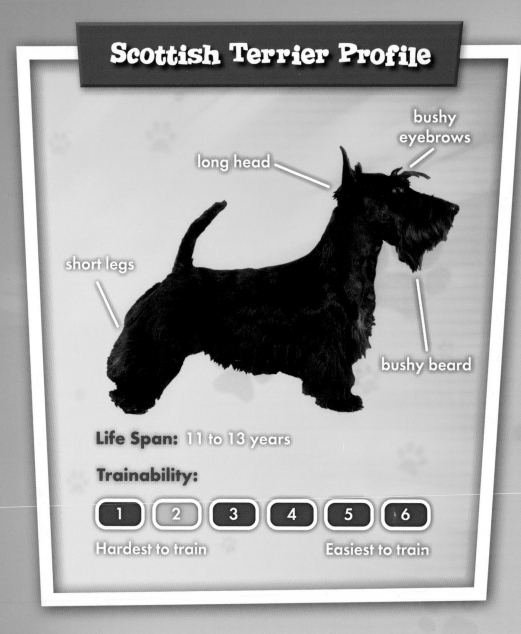

Scottish Terrier Profile

long head

bushy eyebrows

short legs

bushy beard

Life Span: 11 to 13 years

Trainability:

1 2 3 4 5 6

Hardest to train   Easiest to train

Scotties have short legs and thick, raised tails. Pointed ears stand on their long heads.

Scotties look very **serious**. Their eyes are small and bright. **Bushy** beards and eyebrows complete this look.

This **breed** has a thick double **coat**. The top layer is hard and **wiry**.

8

The fur underneath is very soft.

Many Scotties have black fur.
Others are **brindle** or **wheaten**.

Scottish Terrier Coats

brindle   black   wheaten

Some Scottie coats are sprinkled with white or silver hairs.

History of Scottish Terriers

Scottish terriers are from Scotland.

Scotland

N
W E
S

The tough little dogs helped farmers hunt pests. Scotties dug through **burrows** to catch animals like rats and foxes.

Scotties have an unclear history. People confused them with other dogs for many years. The breed's true qualities were decided in 1880.

Scotties soon joined the **Terrier Group** of the **American Kennel Club**.

Today, Scotties are popular pets.
They are smart and **independent**.

These dogs are **loyal**, but they like to do things their own way.

Scotties can be bossy with other pets and small children.

They are not very interested in strangers. But they love their families.

Scottish terriers are very active. They like to go for long walks. Some do **agility**.

This bold breed never backs down!

Glossary

agility—a dog sport where dogs run through a series of obstacles

American Kennel Club—an organization that keeps track of dog breeds in the United States

breed—a type of dog

brindle—a solid coat color mixed with streaks or spots of another color

burrows—holes or tunnels that some animals dig in the ground

bushy—thick and full

coat—the hair or fur covering an animal

independent—able and willing to do things alone

loyal—having constant support for someone

serious—thoughtful or quiet in appearance or manner

sturdy—strongly built

Terrier Group—a group of dog breeds originally bred for hunting mice and other small animals

wheaten—a pale yellow color

wiry—stiff and rough

To Learn More

AT THE LIBRARY

Hansen, Grace. *Scottish Terriers.*
Minneapolis, Minn.: Abdo Kids, 2017.

Rustad, Martha E. H. *Scottish Terriers.* Mankato,
Minn.: Amicus High Interest/Amicus Ink, 2018.

Sommer, Nathan. *West Highland White Terriers.*
Minneapolis, Minn.: Bellwether Media, 2018.

ON THE WEB

Learning more about
Scottish terriers is as
easy as 1, 2, 3.

1. Go to www.factsurfer.com.

2. Enter "Scottish terriers" into the search box.

3. Click the "Surf" button and you will see a
   list of related web sites.

With factsurfer.com, finding more
information is just a click away.

Index

The images in this book are reproduced through the courtesy of: Anna Tkach, front cover, pp. 4-5, 20-21; Eric Isselee, pp. 4-5; Linn Currie, pp. 6, 12; Pavel Shlykov, p. 7; cynoclub, pp. 8-9; Olga_i, pp. 9, 17; Shalyapin Ivan, pp. 10-11; Elisabeth Hammerschmid, p. 11 (left); Kasefoto, p. 11 (center); Nathan Clifford, p. 11 (right); echo1, pp. 12-13; wikicommons, p. 14; Ksenia Merenkova, p. 15; Robert Wedderburn, pp. 16-17; Vikulin, p. 18; Imgorthand, p. 19; Jaanus Järva/ Alamy, pp. 20-21.